A BILLIONAIRE'S LOVE

THE SHERBROOKES OF NEWPORT

CHRISTINA TETREAULT

A Billionaire's Love, ©2020 by Christina Tetreault
Published by Christina Tetreault
Cover Designer: Amanda Walker
Editing: Hot Tree Editing

All rights reserved. No part of this book may be reproduced in any form or by any electronic or mechanical means, including information storage and retrieval systems—except in the case of brief quotations embodied in critical articles or reviews—without permission in writing from the author. This book is a work of fiction. The characters, events, and places portrayed in this book are products of the author's imagination and are either fictitious or are used fictitiously. Any similarity to real persons, living or dead, is purely coincidental and not intended by the author. For more information on the author and her works, please see www.christinatetreault.com

Digital ISBN: 978-1-7352976-3-7

Print ISBN: 978-1-7352976-5-1

Dear Reader,

Those of you who have read all of my books know that once characters get their Happily Ever After, they will occasionally pop up in another book, but I don't give many details about their day-to-day lives. That is why when I sat down to write this novella, I had two goals in mind. First, I wanted to give readers a glimpse at Taylor and Curt's life since we last saw them in *The Billionaire Next Door*.

My second goal was to invite you to a Sherbrooke wedding. Although you attended Trent and Addie's reception in *More than A Billionaire*, Courtney and Josh's reception in *Tempting A Billionaire*, and the prewedding activities in Gray and Kiera's wedding in *The Billionaire Next Door*, you have only witnessed two wedding ceremonies over the past eight years. In case you're asking yourself "which ceremonies did I see," I'll tell you. You were all invited to Dylan and Callie's wedding at the end of *The Teacher's Billionaire*. Later you were present for Jake and Charlie's private ceremony in *The Billionaire Princess*.

In my opinion, I accomplished both goals in *A Billionaire's Love*. Not only that, I think Taylor and Curt's ceremony might be my favorite of all.

I hope you enjoy catching up with everyone as much as I did, and if you have a moment, let me know whose wedding ceremony was your favorite.

Happy Reading
    Christina

ONE

AS CURT LISTENED to the attorney he'd contacted to explain the probable timeline, he pulled the painters' tape off the wood trim around the bedroom window. He'd done so much painting over the past few years, he rarely used it these days. If he'd done all the work in here alone, he wouldn't have used it over the weekend either, but he'd had a nine-year-old helper painting the room.

"Are there any other questions I can answer for you?" Christian asked.

Not wanting to simply do an internet search for adoption attorneys in New Hampshire, Curt had called his cousin Derek, an attorney in Providence, yesterday. Although Derek didn't practice in New Hampshire, he knew plenty of attorneys who did. Within a matter of a few hours, Derek had called him back with Christian Stratford's name and number. According to Derek's contacts, there wasn't anyone better than Christian in the state when it came to adoptions and family law. And first thing this morning, he'd called the office and left a message with the man's secretary. Christian had called him back about an hour ago, and they'd been speaking ever since.

"No, I think you answered all the ones I have for now." Tossing the tape in the trash bag, he gave Honey, the yellow lab he'd adopted in September, a scratch behind the ears before he started removing the tape from around another window.

"Do you want me to start the process?"

The word yes almost slipped out of his mouth because there wasn't a doubt in his mind that he wanted to adopt Reese. In all the ways that mattered, he already considered the girl his daughter and had for a while now. However, before he gave the lawyer the green light, he needed to discuss it with Taylor. While he didn't expect any objections from his fiancée, it was a conversation they needed to have because, as Reese's legal guardian, she had the final say in the matter. Actually, she wasn't the only one he planned to talk to. Reese might only be nine, but it seemed only right that he asked her if she wanted to legally be his daughter and take his last name. Again, much like with his fiancée, he didn't expect any objections, but he'd been wrong in the past.

"Not just yet." He'd spent most of the past month thinking about it, so another few days wouldn't make a difference. "But I'll be in touch soon, either way."

"Sounds good. I'll be here when you're ready. And if you think of any other questions or if your fiancée wants to speak with me, just call."

"I will, thank you."

Curt finished pulling the tape from the second window and stepped into the center of the bedroom. Sometime in July, he'd completed the renovations in his office and his bedroom. With those two areas out of the way, he'd turned his attention to getting a room ready for Reese. And since she'd be calling it her bedroom for at least the next nine or ten years, he'd let her first pick which of the five empty bedrooms she wanted, and then he'd included her in as much of the remodeling process as possible. Although compared to some of the other rooms in the home, the one she picked had required little aside from refinishing the hardwood floors, new light fixtures, and a fresh coat of paint.

Regardless, he'd made some significant changes; the most substantial of which had been converting the extra office located between this room and another bedroom into a bathroom. Although Reese would have to share the bathroom if he and Taylor ever had children and they moved into the room on the other side of the bathroom, at least for the time being, she'd have it all to herself—a situation she was looking forward to. The other major change he'd made had been at Reese's request. Her best friend, Hazel, had a window seat in her bedroom. Naturally, when he and Reese began discussing plans for her new room, she'd asked if he could build her a window seat too. For better or worse, he found it difficult to say no whenever Reese asked for anything—not that she did it often, which was probably a good thing. It'd required some creative thinking, but he'd managed to build her one that also doubled as extra storage and had two built-in bookcases on either side of it. The girl was an avid reader and owned more books than many adults.

While he would've chosen a different color for the walls, overall, he was pleased with the way the room turned out. More importantly, Reese loved it. Not only had she told him as much, but he'd overheard her telling Hazel how great it was and how she couldn't wait to show her while he was driving the two girls home from soccer practice last week. He suspected she'd love the room even more when her new furniture arrived on Thursday and after they put the decals she'd picked out on the walls, which was something he expected her to ask if they could do tonight when he picked her up from soccer practice. She'd asked to do it on Sunday afternoon as soon as they finished painting. If she brought it up, he'd let her get started after she finished her homework.

Since Reese's winter soccer league had started, he'd been picking her and Hazel up from practice on Tuesdays and Thursdays. Unlike the team she played for in the fall and spring, which practiced only in town and not until about five o'clock, her winter team started its practice after school at an indoor sporting complex about twenty minutes away. If the coach had held practices any other days, his future mother-in-law could've gotten Reese to and from soccer practice, but back in September, her schedule had changed. Now she worked at the library on Tuesdays and Thursdays until it closed at seven. Rather than force Reese to quit the team, they'd arranged for Hazel's mom to bring the girls to practice, and then he picked them up. And if he hoped to make it to the sports facility on time, he needed to leave now.

A chilly thirty-five degrees greeted him when he stepped out of his car. It was the first time he'd been outside all day. With his and Taylor's wedding so close, he wanted the initial draft of his current manuscript finished before they left for their honeymoon —a manuscript he'd hoped to be much farther along with by now. But between wedding preparations and assisting with his uncle's reelection campaign, he'd fallen behind. Now he had to play catch-up, an activity he hated, because whenever he felt rushed, the creative side of his brain often went on strike. So far, writer's block hadn't struck, and he had his fingers crossed it wouldn't. Especially since not long after they returned from their honeymoon, they were taking Reese to the theme parks in Florida for a week.

The temperature inside the facility wasn't much better than the one outside. He'd learned from watching many of Reese's games last winter that either the HVAC system in the complex was insufficient for the building's size or it needed additional insulation. More than once, he and Taylor had kept their winter jackets on while they watched Reese play.

Several other parents, many he'd come to know, already sat on the bleachers waiting for practice to end, and he didn't hesitate to join them.

"Do you think they'll finish on time tonight?" William, the father of one of Reese's teammates, asked, glancing over at him. Unlike some of the other girls Reese played with in the winter, William's daughter was also on Reese's town travel team, so of all the parents there, Curt knew him the best.

Coach Bruno and his assistant coach did an excellent job with the girls, but when it came to keeping track of time, forget it. If Curt knew the man better, he'd suggest the coach set a timer, so he knew when to end the practice.

"Last week they managed to on Thursday night, so it's possible. But I wouldn't bet on it."

William gestured toward the field. "It's crazy how much Reese has improved in the past few weeks."

Curt watched Reese in goal, a somewhat new position for her. In the past, she'd always preferred to play the position of striker, but after spending time with his sister's stepdaughter, who loved to play goalie, she'd asked her coach if she could give it a try. Now, it was one of her favorite positions, and she seemed to get better at it every time he saw her play it.

"By the time the spring season starts, she's going to be better than both Hannah and Cassidy," William continued, referring to the two primary goalies on their other team.

Pride surged through him. "A lot of that is thanks to Coach Laurie. Reese told me that for the first thirty minutes of practice on Thursdays, Coach Laurie works with her and the other two goalies. She's also been practicing at home whenever she can get someone to kick balls at her."

"The RedHawks should do the same thing. I don't think the goalies get any specific training."

Out on the turf, the coach blew his whistle, ending the scrimmage on the field. Like most afternoons, the girls took their time getting to the sideline. From what he'd observed, every practice was about socializing as much as it was soccer. All the girls spent whatever time they could talking and joking around. He'd played enough team sports to know comradery amongst players helped make a better team, but some nights he just wanted to leave as soon as Coach Bruno ended the practice. And once Reese and Hazel started talking to their friends, some of whom they didn't go to school with and only saw here, it was hard to get them out of the building.

"They ended on time twice in a row. Maybe Coach Bruno is turning over a new leaf," William said as he stood. "If I don't remind Malory we need to pick up her sister, she'll sit over there all night. I'll see you on Thursday."

While Reese's mouth looked to be going a mile a minute, she and Hazel both had their backpacks on and were walking toward the bleachers. At least tonight, it didn't look like they'd need any extra prodding to get them out of the building.

"Hey, girls. How was practice?"

"Awesome. I scored two goals during our scrimmage," Hazel answered first. Unlike Reese, who'd been playing soccer since she was a toddler, Hazel had only started in the spring. And until today, she'd never scored a goal in a game or at practice.

"That's great. Congratulations." He gave her a high five. "How was practice for you, short stuff?"

"Good. I didn't let any balls into the goal. Coach Bruno said he might let me play keeper for the first half of our game on Saturday."

At some point since he'd walked inside, it'd started raining. Others might disagree, but there wasn't anything much worse than rain on a chilly day. Without being told, the girls sprinted for his car, and Curt followed.

"I told Hazel you're related to the president and that I've been to the White House, but she doesn't believe me. Can you tell her I'm not making it up?" Reese asked as she buckled her seat belt.

He'd never asked, and Reese never brought it up, but he'd assumed she'd told her best friend a long time ago that President

Sherbrooke was his uncle and that she'd spent time with the man on several occasions. The most recent being earlier this month, when they'd attended a family gathering at the White House to celebrate Uncle Warren's reelection.

"Reese is telling you the truth, Hazel. President Sherbrooke is my uncle. And Reese did go to the White House earlier this month."

"See. I told you I was telling the truth."

Even without turning around, he knew there was a triumphant smile on Reese's face. He could hear it in her voice.

"My uncle Thomas is my mom's brother. If President Sherbrooke is your uncle, does that mean he's your mom's brother?" Hazel asked.

"No, Uncle Warren and my dad are brothers."

"Cool. What's it like at the White House? Does it really have a bowling alley inside? Mrs. Andrews, my second-grade teacher, had a book about the White House. One picture showed a bowling alley. I'd love to have one in my house."

He'd made more than one visit to the White House during the four years Uncle Warren had been calling it home, but he'd only used the bowling alley once. Curt had done it more so he could say he'd bowled in the White House, something few people ever got the opportunity to do, than because he loved the activity.

"It does, but it's not big like Willow Tree Lanes." He and Taylor had taken Reese and Hazel to the popular bowling alley in Windham on more than one occasion. "And there are no video games down there."

"The White House also has a game room and a movie theater," Reese added. "I got to watch a movie there with Aunt Taylor and Curt."

He'd noticed she'd been far more impressed by the movie theater than the bowling alley.

"Really? Can I come with you guys the next time you go?" Hazel asked.

You had to ask. Curt liked Hazel. She had a personality much like Reese's, and she was always polite. He hated to disappoint her, but at the same time, he didn't want to lie. "Probably not. They don't allow a lot of visitors into the White House. Reese was only able to go because her aunt and I are engaged."

"That stinks. I'd love to see the bowling alley and meet President Sherbrooke. Mom said he's the best president we've had in a long time."

Curt agreed and would've even if the man wasn't his uncle.

"He might come to Curt and Aunt Taylor's wedding. The First Lady too. Maybe you can meet him then," Reese said.

Although they'd decided to keep the wedding as small as possible, when Reese asked if she could invite Hazel, they'd agreed. According to the RSVP, Hazel's mom and stepdad were accompanying her rather than her dad and stepmother, a fact that pleased both him and Taylor since neither of them cared for Hazel's stepmom. Actually, not even Reese like her friend's stepmom, and she liked everyone.

"Is he *really* going to be at your wedding, Curt?" Hazel asked.

"It's possible."

His uncle tried to attend every wedding and major family event he could. Since Uncle Warren first took office, he'd only missed three of the ten weddings that had taken place, and one of them he'd missed simply because Curt's cousin Jake had a secret wedding in Hawaii to avoid a media frenzy and hadn't invited his parents.

"I hope he comes. It'd be so cool to tell the kids at school I met the President of the United States."

At Hazel's age, he would've been far more eager to meet his favorite baseball player than a politician, but to each their own. "If he comes, I'll make sure you meet him and the First Lady, my aunt Elizabeth." Curt pulled into Hazel's driveway and put the car in park.

"Awesome. I'll text you after dinner, Reese," she said, opening the car door. "Thanks for the ride home, Curt."

He waited until Hazel's mom opened the door and the girl went inside before backing out of the driveway. And once they were back on the road, Reese launched into what he'd dubbed "411 mode" and gave him every detail about her day at school, including the fact that Justin, Hazel's cousin, threw up in the middle of gym class—a detail he could've done without, but when Reese filled you in on her day, she didn't leave anything out.

"Can we put the soccer decals on my bedroom walls?" She didn't even bother to remove her jacket before asking the question when they entered his house. "You said the paint would be dry by today."

He knew her teacher's routine. Every Monday, Mrs. Wilson sent the students home with a packet of work, which was due on Friday. Students could do it all at once or a little each night. She didn't care, as long as they turned it in on Friday. If it'd been up to him, he would've let Reese decide how she wanted to tackle the weekly assignment. Taylor, on the other hand, insisted Reese do a little each night. Since she was the one in charge, he made sure Reese completed one assignment before she did anything else when she stayed with him after school.

"Homework first. You know that. While you do that, I'll start dinner, and when you're done, I'll help you if you want."

In addition to picking up Reese on Tuesdays and Thursdays, he also prepared dinner for the three of them. Although it wasn't uncommon for Taylor to leave work late, and then they ate without her.

Reese's sigh almost knocked him over, but she sat down at the kitchen table and pulled out her school folder. "I'm going to do the math tonight."

"Really? You always save math until the end. Are you feeling okay, short stuff?" The girl treated her math assignments similar to the way most people treated snakes. She always avoided it for as long as possible and didn't even look at it until Thursdays.

"We're going over how to multiply double-digit numbers. It's super easy because Aunt Taylor taught me how to do it last year."

He interpreted her statement to mean she'd zip through her work tonight, and then they could hang the decals.

"What are we having for dinner?" Reese asked as she flipped through pages in her homework packet.

"Steak and baked potatoes." While they'd improved considerably since he moved here, compared to Taylor's and Priscilla's, his culinary skills were somewhat lacking. However, he excelled at grilling, and he did it regardless of whether it was raining or there were several feet of snow on the ground.

"Yes, steak!"

He'd expected such a reaction. The girl loved meat, especially steak and burgers.

TWO

IF TAYLOR never stepped foot in another high-end women's clothing store until after she retired, it'd still be too soon. More than once, Taylor had insisted Judith, Curt's mom, didn't need to consult her on what she wore to the wedding. Actually, she'd told Mom the same thing when she asked not only for Taylor to go shopping with her but also to help her make the final decision. Much like Mom, though, Judith dismissed her comments.

Still, she'd delayed the shopping trip with Curt's mom for as long as possible in the hope Judith would get tired of waiting and either go alone or perhaps with her daughter or one of her nieces. It wasn't that she didn't like Curt's mom or enjoy spending time with her. Taylor genuinely liked Judith. From the very first day they'd met, she'd been nothing but friendly, and she treated Reese like a granddaughter. If Judith wanted her to accompany her almost anywhere else, Taylor would have been happy to. But she hated shopping. Whenever possible, Taylor ordered what she or Reese needed from the internet. Heck, she even ordered deodorant in bulk from the internet to avoid shopping in stores.

She'd finally caved to Judith's requests last week. And today, as promised, Taylor left work early and met her on Newbury Street, the home to some of the most exclusive stores in Boston. Before they even left the first store, Taylor wished she'd suggested to Curt that they either elope or get married at the town hall with just her mom, Reese, and his parents in attendance with a nice dinner at her favorite Italian restaurant afterward. If they'd taken either of those two routes, she could've escaped weeks of shopping for everything from the perfect wedding gown to a pretty junior bridesmaid dress for Reese, a task that had been almost as difficult as finding the perfect location for the reception, because Reese hated wearing dresses.

Thankfully, today's shopping trip was a success, and fingers crossed, except for her final dress fitting, she wouldn't need to step foot in another clothing store for a long time. Although considering Reese's current growth spurt, she might need to purchase the girl a whole new wardrobe when she and Curt returned from their honeymoon. Already some of the jeans she'd bought Reese in August right before school started were getting too short. But she wouldn't worry about future trips to the mall, shopping, or even work anymore tonight.

"Where is everyone?" Taylor called out after entering Curt's home. By now, Reese would have finished with her homework. Curt always made sure she tackled it right after soccer practice. So if she had to guess, she'd say the two of them were upstairs working on Reese's bedroom, or Reese was in the living room reading. Her niece devoured books. After playing soccer and, more recently, lacrosse, reading was her favorite activity. Occasionally, when she got here on Tuesdays and Thursdays, she'd find Reese and Curt in the living room either playing video games or watching a movie. Curt had plenty of both on hand that were age appropriate for Reese. But it didn't happen often.

"I'm in the kitchen." Curt's voice reached her in the foyer.

If he was in the kitchen, most likely, Reese had her nose buried in a book. And when she got lost in a story, she hated to be pulled out, and Taylor tried not to do so unless she had to. Rather than go in search of Reese, she turned down the hall toward the kitchen.

She found Curt at the counter. Stepping up behind him and putting a hand on his shoulder, Taylor kissed his cheek. "Hey, you."

Rather than give her a chance to ask about his day or what Reese was up to, Curt turned, put his arms around her, and kissed her.

Lifting his lips from hers, he smiled. "I'm glad you're home."

Although she and Reese didn't technically live there yet and wouldn't for a couple more weeks, on multiple occasions, Curt told them he wanted them both to consider this home. In the beginning, she'd found it a little awkward. She'd only ever called two places home: the apartment she'd lived in for a short time in Boston before becoming Reese's guardian and her parents' house where she'd grown up and had been living again for the past several years. Reese hadn't suffered from the same feelings. She'd taken Curt's words to heart and acted the same way here as she did next door. And that even included leaving her shoes in the middle of the living room floor for people to trip over.

"Did you and Mom find a dress?"

"Yep." She stepped out of his embrace and opened a cabinet door. "Fingers crossed, except for finishing the seating arrangement and my last dress fitting, everything for the wedding is done."

Not long after they'd first met, she'd attended his cousin Gray's wedding in Newport. Even though they'd left before the ceremony actually started, she'd seen the number of guests in attendance. So, from the moment she accepted Curt's proposal, she'd prepared herself for a lot of negotiating because her ideal wedding didn't involve having hundreds of guests on hand.

In the end, the only thing they'd negotiated on was the menu for the reception, because Curt suggested they have a small, or at least small by Sherbrooke standards, wedding from the start. Rather than invite every acquaintance he and his family had like many of his cousins had done, they'd only added his aunts and uncles as well as his cousins and a handful of friends to the guest list. She hadn't blinked an eye at his suggestion to include his cousins. In the year and a half they'd been together, she had spent enough time around his family to know how close he was to all of them.

Taylor poured a can of soda water into her glass before adding a splash of cranberry juice. "Where's Reese?"

"Living room. Right after she finished putting the decals up in her room, she grabbed a book from her backpack and disappeared in there. I haven't seen or heard from her since." Curt moved to the other side of the kitchen and opened the oven. "But dinner is done if you want to get her."

Taylor didn't need to hear that twice. Her stomach was in the process of eating itself, and the sooner she got food into it, the better.

TAYLOR NEVER COMPLAINED when Curt grilled. Actually, she never complained when he cooked because she was glad to be able to come home at night and not worry about making a meal for her and Reese. However, Taylor much preferred when he prepared dinner on the grill. Maybe it was just her, but she found almost everything tasted better when cooked that way, including most veggies. The steaks he'd made tonight were as delicious as always. The same was true of the portobello mushrooms he cooked on the grill and the oven-roasted rosemary potatoes.

What had been unlike usual, though, was Curt himself. After

being together for over a year and a half, she could read him. And the look he'd worn tonight, she'd seen countless times. While he contributed a little to the conversation, his mind had been elsewhere. More than likely, it'd been on his current manuscript. He'd helped a lot during his uncle's campaign and had fallen behind. Ever since election day, he'd been playing catch-up, so he'd meet his deadline.

Taylor turned on the dishwasher and returned to the table. "Did you hit another snag with the book?"

Except for in the most general terms, although she asked about them, they didn't discuss his writing projects with Reese around. While his novels weren't X-rated or anything, they were suspense books and included some violence. But with Reese once again in the living room reading, they were alone for the moment.

"No, I got a lot accomplished today. I should finish it on time."

"Oh, then is something else wrong? You weren't exactly mentally here during dinner." Prior to her relationship with Curt, she hadn't realized how beneficial talking to someone could be when something bothered you. And since he shared everything with her as well, she guessed he found it just as helpful.

"Sorry. Nothing's wrong. But there's something I want to talk to you about."

"Go for it. I'm listening."

Resting both his elbows on the table, Curt clasped his hands together. "You know I love Reese like a daughter. I can't even imagine my life without the two of you."

If this was what he wanted to discuss, there was no need. She knew how Curt felt about Reese. From the very beginning of their relationship, he'd showered her niece with love and attention. And in all the ways that mattered, he acted like Reese's dad. "I know how much you love her, Curt. So does she." Not only did Reese know how Curt felt about her, but she loved him too.

"I want to adopt her. I'd like to legally be her father and for her to take my last name," he explained.

Taylor considered herself an astute individual. However, she'd never expected to be having this conversation with Curt. Instead, she'd assumed the only thing that would really change after they got married was where she and Reese lived—at least until they had children. Yet here they were, and once again, she wondered how she'd gotten so lucky.

"Obviously, I want to adopt her because I love her, but it's not the only reason." Curt continued while she processed his previous statement. "If she's my daughter when we have children, they will be her siblings. And if something ever happened to you, legally, there would be no question about who would take care of her."

She wondered how long he'd been considering this decision because clearly he'd put a lot of thought into it.

He didn't give her a chance to offer an opinion or ask a question. "This afternoon, I spoke with an attorney. According to him, since you are her legal guardian, the adoption process would be more or less the same as if you were her biological mother and I wanted to adopt her after we got married. He said it wouldn't take long." He reached into his pocket and pulled out a slip of paper. "The attorney's name is Christian Stratford. He specializes in family law and adoptions. He said you can call him anytime if you have any questions."

Taylor glanced down at the slip of paper Curt held, but she didn't reach for it.

"You don't have to decide today or even this week. But if you agree, I'd like to get the process going as soon as possible."

If he'd given her a chance to talk, he'd already have his answer. "Can I speak now?"

He set the paper with the name and number down in front of

A BILLIONAIRE'S LOVE

her. "Yeah, of course, but you don't have to make a decision now. It's not like I'm going to change my mind. And no matter what you decide, it won't change how I feel about Reese."

Under the table, she nudged his foot with hers. "You said I could get a word into this conversation, so zip it."

Curt pretended to pull a zipper across his lips and then toss an imaginary key over his shoulder as if he was a kid.

"There's nothing for me to think about. I love the idea. I kind of wish I'd suggested it to you. Whenever you're ready to get the ball rolling, let me know, and I'll do whatever you need me to."

He pretended to tug at the end of a zipper.

"Yes, you can speak again."

That was all he needed to hear before he unzipped the imaginary zipper keeping his lips closed. But before he managed a single syllable, Taylor placed her index finger over his mouth.

"I love you." She should have told him so right after he announced his desire to adopt Reese, but better late than never.

"I'm—"

She didn't allow him to finish. "Did you seriously think I would say no?"

Grabbing the back of her chair, he pulled it and her closer to him. "For the most part, I expected you to agree, but I knew you might have some reason why you'd rather keep the situation between you and Reese as it is."

And you might need to have your head examined sometime soon. Considering the seriousness of their conversation, she refrained from sharing the thought. "What's the first step?"

"Talking to Reese. I want to make sure she wants me as her father."

She expected something more along the lines of having a meeting with the attorney. "You're kidding, right? Reese loves you, and I am pretty sure she considers you her father now. There is no way she won't want you to adopt her."

Her niece had never said she viewed Curt that way, but her

actions did. She'd even given Curt the Father's Day gift she'd made in school back in June. Ever since Reese started making such gifts in school, she'd always given them to her. This year, she'd insisted Curt get the present.

"You're probably right." He reached for her hand and laced their fingers together. "But I still want to ask her. I think she deserves a say in the matter."

She didn't doubt for a moment that Reese would agree. Still, she couldn't fault him for wanting to ask Reese her opinion. "Do you want to talk to her tonight before we go home, or would you rather wait?"

Taylor liked to get Reese into bed by eight on school nights, not that her niece went to sleep then. Most nights, Reese stayed up for at least a half an hour reading. It was already closing in on seven thirty, so any conversation needed to take place soon.

"I'd like to do it tonight. And if she says yes, I can call Christian back in the morning. But if you want me to wait until we have more time, I'll talk to her about it tomorrow."

Since Taylor expected an immediate yes, Curt could get the answer he wanted, and she could still get Reese home and into bed on time. "Do it tonight. I'll go get her."

She found Reese curled up in her favorite oversized armchair in the living room. Reese loved it so much that Curt had purchased one, just in a different color, for Reese's bedroom at his house. It would arrive this week along with the rest of the furniture Curt and Reese picked out—furniture Taylor had insisted Reese didn't need. Her niece had a perfectly good bedroom set at home. Instead of buying an entire room's worth of furniture, she suggested he let Reese pick out a few extras such as a desk or some bookcases, since her new bedroom was much larger than her current one. He'd disagreed. He'd argued that finding pieces to match what she already had would be difficult. Curt had also pointed out Reese would need someplace to sleep when she had overnights with her grandmother. At least on that account, she'd had a counter-argument. Even if they moved Reese's furniture over, hers would remain, and Reese could easily sleep in Taylor's old room.

In the end, Curt took Reese shopping and, not surprisingly, let her pick out whatever she wanted. The man loved to spoil her niece.

"How's the book?" Taylor asked, stopping alongside the chair. Reese had started the book she was reading last night. It was the third in a five-book series.

Reese didn't even look up from the paperback. "Okay. The first one is still my favorite."

Taylor had read none of the books, so she didn't have an opinion. "Curt wants to talk to you before we leave. He's waiting for you in the kitchen."

"Can I finish this chapter first? I only have four more pages."

"Nope, what he wants to talk to you about is important. You can finish the chapter when you go up to bed."

With a sigh only a nine-year-old could conjure, she rolled her eyes as she stuck the bookmark between the pages and stood up. "Do you know what Curt wants?"

"Yep, and I think it's going to make you very happy." No way was she spoiling Curt's surprise.

Taylor's personal cell phone rang as they entered the kitchen, and she pulled the device from her pocket rather than retake her seat at the table. Unlike her work phone issued by the DEA, few people called her private number, so even before she looked, she expected to see the name Mom on the screen.

"Hi, Mom. Is something wrong?"

Mom was familiar with their Tuesday night routine, which meant she knew they'd be home soon. If she was calling, perhaps she'd gotten another flat tire. She'd gotten one last month, and rather than wait for the auto club to come and change it, Curt had driven over to the library and done it for her.

"I need you to come home. If Curt's not busy, it might be good if he comes too."

Mom's statement sent Taylor's memory back to the single worst moment in her life: the day Eliza, Reese's biological mother, and Eliza's boyfriend abducted Reese from a friend's birthday party while Taylor was in Newport with Curt at his cousin's wedding.

Without thinking, she placed a hand on Reese's shoulder. "Why? What happened?"

Taylor had a handful of aunts and uncles as well as several cousins, although she was only close to a few of them. Something might have happened to one of them and Mom wanted to tell her. But if she'd received bad news regarding a family member, why did she want Curt to come over as well?

Curt and Reese looked at her, but both remained silent.

"Not long after I got home, I received a phone call from one of your sister's friends."

Taylor closed her eyes and pinched the bridge of her nose. She didn't need to hear any more. "We'll be right home."

Considering the type of people her sister had hung around with before going back to prison, she could only imagine the conversation her mom had moments ago. She shoved her cell phone back into her pocket. "Reese, Mimi needs to talk to me. Please go get your things."

"But Curt wants to talk to me, remember."

"I know, but he'll have to do it later. Go get your stuff so that we can go home."

Remarkably without any more questions, Reese left the room.

"What's wrong?" Standing, Curt came around the table.

"Mom got a phone call from one of Eliza's friends."

Although she'd suggested they get rid of the landline, Mom insisted on keeping it and the phone number she'd had for over thirty years. According to her, you never knew when you might need it.

"One of your sister's friends called Priscilla. What the hell did they want?" A combination of disbelief and anger filled his voice.

Taylor shared the same emotions as Curt. "Mom didn't go into details. She only asked me to come home and said it might be a good idea if you come over too."

"Of course. Let's go."

THREE

THE WEDDING MIGHT BE a few weeks away, but Curt already considered Taylor, Reese, and Priscilla a part of his family, and he'd do anything for them. And at the moment, he wanted to track down whoever had called Taylor's mom and make sure they knew never to do it again.

Priscilla never mentioned her eldest daughter. Still, he knew the life choices Eliza had made and her current incarceration weighed heavily on his future mother-in-law. And he didn't blame her. Regardless of the things Eliza had done, she was still Priscilla's daughter. It couldn't be easy to see someone you love make such terrible decisions. The last thing Taylor's mom needed was one of Eliza's friends calling her.

They found Priscilla seated in the kitchen frowning and drumming her fingers on the table with what looked like an untouched cup of tea. When she spotted Reese, though, she forced a smile and pushed back her chair.

"Hey, sweetie. How was your day?" Priscilla asked, hugging her granddaughter.

"School was boring, but Coach Bruno might let me play goalie first on Saturday. And Curt wanted to talk to me about something that Aunt Taylor said would make me happy, but we came home before he could."

"That's my fault. I'm sorry. I needed to see Aunt Taylor and Curt. But I'm sure Curt will have that conversation with you soon."

"Reese, go on up and get ready for bed and read. I'll be up to tuck you in later," Taylor said.

Reese retrieved her book from her backpack and hugged first Taylor, then him. "Will you come up and say good night before you leave?"

As if she needed to ask. "Of course."

Happy with his answer, she zipped out of the kitchen.

"Okay, Mom. What's going on?" Taylor asked as they both sat down at the table.

"About five minutes after I walked in the door, the house phone rang. I almost didn't answer it." Priscilla reached for her tea but then clasped her hands together again. "For some reason, I did. The man introduced himself as Jordan King, and he said he was a friend of Eliza."

Under the table, Taylor's leg rubbed against his as she bounced her foot on the floor. He shared her impatience. At the moment, he cared more about what the caller wanted than what their name was or the moments leading up to the call.

"He claimed he got a letter recently from Eliza. In it, she told him he might be Reese's father. She included our phone number so he could contact us."

Taylor pushed back her chair with so much force it almost tipped over and stalked across the kitchen. When she reached the counter, she turned and raked her hand through her hair. "That doesn't make sense."

"When did anything your sister does make sense?" Priscilla asked, stealing the words right out of his thoughts. "The fact that she was sleeping around so much she didn't know who Reese's father was in the first place is a perfect example of her poor decision making."

He'd never heard the older woman sound so bitter.

"But why now? She's had more than nine years to contact this guy or the other men who might be Reese's father, Mom."

Curt had his suspicions on that, but he didn't plan to share.

"Do you need to ask that?" Priscilla nodded toward him, and Curt suspected their thoughts were flowing in the same direction. "Eliza blames you and Curt for her being in prison."

Taylor rejoined them at the table, and he took her hand. "How do you know that? Neither of us has communicated with her since her arrest."

"That's not entirely true. I didn't reply to either, but I've received two letters from your sister. She mentioned you and Curt in both. Eliza believes if you'd given her and Brad the money as they asked, she wouldn't be where she is. And she knows you and Curt are getting married. Most of the country knows it. Telling this man he might be Reese's father might be her way of getting back at the two of you."

"Why—never mind. What does this guy want?"

"If he wants money to go away, I'll write him a check tomorrow." Curt knew nothing about the man, but if he'd spent time with Eliza, he doubted he was the type of person who should be around a nine-year-old child.

Priscilla shook her head. "Jordan didn't mention anything about money. He said he wants to find out if he's Reese's father. And if he is, he wants to be involved in her life."

Curt couldn't fault the man. If he'd ever received a similar letter from an ex-girlfriend, he'd want the same thing. Regardless, anger toward Eliza for not thinking of Reese first and fear that this man might be Reese's father ate at him.

"Do you believe Eliza contacted him?" he asked. He recognized the question for what it was, a weak attempt at finding a reason they could dismiss Jordan's claims.

"I wish I could say no, but how else would he have gotten our phone number if not from Eliza?" Priscilla replied.

"How did you leave things with him?" Taylor asked.

"I explained you had custody of Reese, so he'd have to speak with you. He gave me his number and wants you to call him. He wants to meet with you and Reese. And—"

"No."

"Not happening," he said at the same time.

For the first time since they sat down, Priscilla smiled. "I knew you'd both say that."

"I'll meet him. Reese can either stay here or maybe with Curt. And I don't want her to know about this right now. If it turns out to be true, we'll cross that bridge then."

Curt squeezed Taylor's hand to get her attention. "I'll be there when you meet him."

"You don't—"

"Yes, I do."

"I thought you'd both say that too. I promised Jordan I'd pass along his number and that you'd call him soon." Priscilla picked up the cup and took a sip. "I need to heat this up. Do either of you want some tea?"

After this conversation, Curt needed something stronger than tea. But since Taylor and Priscilla didn't drink scotch or bourbon, they didn't keep any in the house. "Sure."

"I'll have some too, Mom." Taylor closed her eyes and rubbed her forehead, a severe frown on her face.

He wanted to tell her everything would be fine. That they'd meet this man and one of two things would happen—either Jordan would turn out not to be Reese's biological father or, if he was, he'd offer to disappear and not claim any parental rights in exchange for money. In the case of the second scenario, Curt would hand over whatever sum the man requested. But he kept his mouth shut because who knew what would happen over the next few days.

"Until we know one way or the other, you can't ask Reese if she wants you to adopt her," Taylor said. "Because if Jordan turns out to be her father, he might make it impossible, and she'd be devastated."

As much as Curt hated it, he'd reached the same conclusion already. "Yeah, I know."

FOUR

TAYLOR HAD WANTED to ignore the message Mom passed along and hope Jordan King didn't call again or, even worse, show up at the house. If Eliza had provided him with their phone number, she might have given him their address as well—not that it'd be all that difficult to find it on the internet, assuming Jordan knew what town they lived in. While she didn't know everyone, she believed they were the only Walkers currently living in Pelham.

As far as she was concerned, Reese had a father now. A man who'd do anything and everything for her. She didn't need some low-life creep suddenly appearing in her life. And Taylor didn't see how Jordan could be anything other than a creep if he had been involved with Eliza. Not to mention Reese had already suffered enough for three lifetimes thanks to Eliza and Brad. Who knew how she might respond if it turned out this stranger was her biological father?

At the same time, though, she suspected Jordan wouldn't simply go away. Whether he genuinely wanted to know if he had a daughter or was after something else, she didn't know, but if Jordan had reached out to them once, he'd most likely do it again.

So although it'd gone against what she wanted, Taylor contacted him Wednesday. Considering the subject of the call and the fact Jordan knew her sister, she'd prepared herself for an unpleasant conversation. While it'd been uncomfortable and awkward, it'd gone far better than she'd expected. After he'd more or less reiterated the details he gave to Mom, Jordan requested a meeting with both her and Reese. When she'd refused to bring Reese along, he hadn't pushed the issue. In fact, he'd said he understood her desire to protect Reese. He'd also agreed to her predetermined location and time for their meeting, something she and Curt discussed in great detail before he left on Tuesday night. On the off chance the man didn't know where they lived, neither of them wanted to invite him into her mom's house. The subject matter, though, made them both leery about having the meeting in a coffee shop or a restaurant. In the end, Curt offered the use of his house. Although not ideal, it would give them the privacy she wanted and didn't potentially give Jordan additional information about Reese.

"I'll need to refinish the floor if you don't sit down," Curt said Saturday afternoon.

Like he could talk. He'd been drumming his fingers against the table for the last ten minutes. "If it needs to be done, I'll help you." She pulled out the chair next to him and sat. She'd invited Jordan over for one o'clock. It was five minutes until then now. If she'd been in Jordan's position, she would've already arrived.

"She gets that habit from her dad," Priscilla explained.

In the beginning, Taylor had planned for only her and Curt to meet with Jordan. After thinking about it, though, it seemed right to include Mom this afternoon.

"Reese played well this morning," Curt said, clearly in an attempt to distract her.

Reese's game had been at ten o'clock today. Like Coach Bruno told her, she'd played keeper first. She hadn't let in a single goal. In the second half of the game, she'd scored one goal, and Hazel had scored the team's other one.

Taylor nodded and rechecked her watch.

"I bet she gave my mom a play-by-play recap of the game in the car," he continued.

Curt's mom had met them at the house after the game and picked Reese up for the rest of the day. Reese hadn't complained about the unexpected outing with Judith. She loved spending time with Curt's mom as much as she did with her grandmother. And if anyone ever saw the two of them together, they'd assume they were a grandmother and granddaughter spending the day together. She'd noticed Curt's mom treated Erin, Leah's stepdaughter, the same way.

"I told Mom not to spoil Reese too much today," Curt said.

Taking a page out of Curt's book, Taylor started tapping her fingertips against the table. "And like Judith always does, she'll ignore you." The word "overboard" didn't exist in Judith's vocabulary.

"Probably, but everyone deserves to get spoiled sometimes."

No sooner did he finish speaking than the doorbell rang. Although she'd been pacing moments ago, Taylor now found her butt glued to the chair. Perhaps everyone else suffered from the same ailment because no one moved a muscle.

"I'll get it." The first to move, Curt pushed his chair back and stood.

Curt's voice broke whatever hold the chair had on her butt, and she stood too. "I should be with you. Mom, maybe you should stay here."

Mom nodded as she took in a deep breath and slowly exhaled.

Based on her sister's past and the type of friends she'd spent time with, Taylor expected to see someone who looked like Brad, Eliza's kidnapping partner last year. The man standing on Curt's front step was about as different from what she expected as one could get. Dressed in jeans and a black leather jacket, Jordan had short, light brown hair and looked as if he took good care of himself.

Why would you ever get involved with my sister? "Jordan?" Taylor asked rather than assume, because for all she knew, the man in front of her wanted to sell them something. After all, a few weeks earlier, a salesman had stopped by their house offering to give them a free estimate on all new windows.

Nodding, the man extended his hand, and again she wondered about how he met Eliza and why he'd ever spent time with her. "It's nice to meet you," Jordan said.

"Please come in." She took several steps back so that he could enter. "Jordan, this is my fiancé, Curt."

"I've seen pictures of you together." As he'd done with her, Jordan shook Curt's hand.

Okay, time to get this over with. As if reading her mind, Curt squeezed her hand. "We'll be more comfortable in the kitchen," she said.

They hadn't discussed what type of man Jordan might be, but the way Mom's eyes grew wide when she saw Jordan walk in the room told Taylor their assumptions had been similar.

"Jordan, this is my mother, Priscilla. I thought she should be here today too."

Before sitting down, Jordan pulled an envelope from his back pocket and removed his jacket, revealing a wrinkle-free, dark green button-down shirt. "I brought the letter Eliza sent me. I thought you might like to see it. Please feel free to read it."

Without hesitation, Taylor accepted the envelope and pulled out the letter. She recognized Eliza's barely legible handwriting right away. It had always been so poor that it'd been common for teachers to make her redo assignments before they even tried to grade them in school.

Eliza had kept the letter short. In it, she didn't ask how Jordan had been or what he'd been up to. Instead, Eliza explained she'd had a baby nine years ago, and she believed he might be her daughter's father. She also mentioned that she'd given up custody to Taylor when Reese was about a year old and then provided him with Taylor and Priscilla's home phone number. Eliza gave no explanation as to why she'd waited so long to reach out or why she felt the need to do so now. Eliza did, however, ask him to write back and let her know if he turned out to be Reese's father.

"Do you want to read it, Mom?" she asked once done.

Mom considered the question before answering. "No. I don't think I do."

Taylor refolded the letter and handed it back. She'd share the contents of it with Curt later. "I'm guessing you never knew Eliza was pregnant when you were together?" She had a lot of questions, and this one seemed as good a place to start as anywhere.

Jordan took a sip from the water Curt had set in front of each of them before joining them at the table. "Eliza and I never had a, uh... exclusive relationship, I guess you'd say." He glanced at her mom and cleared his throat. "Every once in a while, she'd call me and then come over. If she knew she was pregnant the last time we got together, she didn't say anything."

"Then you haven't seen her in over nine years?" Taylor asked.

Jordan shook his head. "About two years ago, I ran into her at the mall in Nashua. I almost didn't recognize her."

Yeah, she could understand that. When Eliza had shown up at the door suddenly a few months before the kidnapping, Taylor had been shocked by the transformation in her sister's appearance.

"She said she would call, but she never did. Honestly, at the time, I was glad she didn't. But yeah, I'd say it's been more than nine years since she was at my house," Jordan explained.

In the long run, it didn't matter, but she wanted to know. "How did you meet my sister?"

"At a party a mutual friend was having."

That made sense. Eliza always loved a party.

"Has Eliza written to anyone else and given them the same news?" Jordan asked.

Great question. Taylor hoped not. If Jordan proved not to be Reese's father, she didn't want to go through this again.

"I'm not sure. I haven't talked to my sister in more than a year. But when Eliza found out she was pregnant, she claimed she had no idea who the father was. I always assumed that meant there were more than two possibilities out there. So it is possible she reached out to more than just you."

"Sounds like Eliza." Jordan clasped his hands together on the table. "As I told you on the phone, I want to know if Reese is my daughter."

"And if she is?" Curt asked.

She wasn't sure who wanted Jordan not to be Reese's father more, her or Curt.

"Then, I want to be a part of her life."

He'd said as much on the phone both when Mom spoke to him and again when they talked. Still, she'd hoped once Jordan had an answer, regardless of the outcome, he'd go away and they'd never hear from him again.

"You do realize that might not be the best thing for Reese," Curt said.

He'd suggested she let him offer Jordan a nice sum to simply forget he ever received the letter and walk away. At the time, she hadn't known if he was serious or not. His tone now erased any doubt. Curt would willingly transfer whatever sum of money it took to get Jordan out the door.

"She's always known only Taylor and Priscilla. Not to mention the trauma she suffered last year at the hands of Eliza.

Reese doesn't need anyone else upsetting her life," Curt continued.

Last night, Curt told her he'd leave this conversation in her hands, that he'd be there mostly for moral support. Either he'd changed his mind or his emotions were getting the better of him.

"I don't know what Eliza did, and I don't intend to take Reese away from Taylor. But if I'm her father, I have the right to be a part of her life. I believe kids do better when they have a mother and a father who play an active role in their lives."

FIVE

"Reese already—" Under the table, Taylor squeezed his thigh, and Curt stopped before he completed his thought. If he became confrontational, it wouldn't help the situation. "I agree. Children often benefit from having more than one parent."

Taylor patted his thigh and then gave Jordan the condensed version of why Eliza once again found herself behind bars. While she did that, he kept his trap shut and listened. Now, like so many other times, Curt wondered how anyone could put their child through what Eliza had.

Jordan's face expressed a similar amount of disbelief and outrage. "I wouldn't have thought Eliza capable of doing that."

Curt wanted to hate the man across from him. At the moment, Jordan stood in the way of what he wanted. Worse than that, though, he could potentially cause upheaval in Reese's life. Despite those two issues, Curt didn't hate Jordan. In fact, in a way, he even sympathized with him. If a paternity test proved Reese was Jordan's biological child, the man had missed out on nine years of his daughter's life. Nine years he could never get back, and all because Eliza hadn't bothered to contact him before or right after giving birth.

"Has Reese suffered any long-term effects from the kidnapping?" Jordan asked, the concern in his voice only making it that much harder for Curt to dislike him.

"Thankfully, she never realized Eliza took her without our permission. She thought we sent her to pick her up that day, so she's unaware of the true severity of what happened," Taylor replied.

They'd all feared the worse when they brought Reese home, and immediately Taylor had taken Reese to a child psychologist for regular therapy sessions. But Reese hadn't seen the therapist in about six or seven months.

"After I got the letter, I did some research. Paternity tests are not invasive. I'd like to have one done soon."

Not only had Curt and Taylor done their fair share of reading, but he'd talked to his cousin. Scott had discovered his oldest child, Cooper, was his via a paternity test after an ex-girlfriend dropped the news that he might be Cooper's father about a month after he was born. So they knew what the test entailed and how long it should take to get results.

"I've already contacted Mass Genetics and set up an appointment to bring Reese to their facility in Boston for a cheek swab. It's on Longwood Avenue. They also have a laboratory in Concord if that one is closer for you," Taylor said, leaving the table.

They'd learned quickly that there were three simple ways to get a paternity test completed. Both individuals could go to a lab and have their cheeks swabbed. If a person didn't have the time to make such a trip, they could order a test from a facility like Mass Genetics, collect the buccal cells found on the inside of the cheek, and then mail it back. The last method and the one he was most uncomfortable with because getting results generally took the longest involved picking up a test at the local pharmacy, doing the cheek swab, and mailing it back in. While any of the methods might have worked for them, they'd agreed that having a professional conduct the test reduced the possibility of human error. While they'd found several facilities in both New Hampshire and Massachusetts, they'd settled on Mass Genetics because they by far had the best reputation. And since they were talking about Reese's future, they wanted the test performed by the best out there. The fact they had a satellite office in New Hampshire was a bonus, since they didn't know where Jordan lived.

When she rejoined them, she tore a piece of paper off the pad and passed it over to Jordan. "Here is the main laboratory's phone number and address. I've already paid for the testing to be completed. The representative I spoke with assured me once they have a sample of cells from both you and Reese, it should only take three to six days to get us the results."

"Monday morning, I'll call and get an appointment as soon as possible." Jordan stuck the paper in his wallet, and Curt hoped that meant he planned to leave. "I understand why you didn't want Reese here, but do you have a picture of her I could see?"

Curt almost said no but stopped himself before the word came out. Although he might think of her as his daughter, at the end of the day, she wasn't, and every decision regarding Reese was up to Taylor. That included whether or not Jordan could see a photo.

Next to him, Taylor picked up her cell phone. Although every cell in his body protested, he couldn't come up with a good reason to suggest Taylor not show Jordan any of the photos stored on her device.

He watched her scroll through the various pictures taken over the summer. Finally, she paused at one his sister took for them at his parents' annual Fourth of July cookout. In it, Reese stood between him and Taylor on the beach; the giant sandcastle they, along with his sister's stepdaughter, had worked on was at their feet, and the ocean was in the background.

Taylor passed the device across the table. "This is from this past July."

Jordan studied the picture and then set the device down on the table. "She looks like Eliza."

Curt had never met Eliza, and Priscilla didn't have any pictures of her oldest daughter displayed in the house. However, both Taylor and Priscilla had told him Reese resembled her mom a lot.

"It was nice meeting you all today," Jordan said, standing and slipping on his jacket.

Wish I could say the same. Curt pushed his chair back, eager to walk his guest to the front door. Next to him, Taylor did the same.

"When I get an appointment at the lab, I'll let you know. I work close to Concord, so I'll call the lab there and see if I can get in this week. If they don't have any openings, I'll set something up in Boston."

Well, that gave them a little more information about the man. But what he'd rather have was a home address so he could have Elite Force Security dig up all there was to know about Jordan King. Even without the address, the firm's cyber division could probably uncover any skeletons in the guy's closet by simply starting with his phone number. There wasn't much the men and women who worked for the firm couldn't do when it came to computers. He'd said as much to Taylor before she called Jordan back to set up today's meeting. She'd told him to hold off until they knew the truth.

Curt again considered asking how much it would take for Jordan to forget he ever received the letter as they walked toward the front door. But he didn't do it. Whatever the paternity test revealed, Reese, Jordan, and Taylor deserved to know the truth.

"I hope you don't mind. I started some coffee," Priscilla called over her shoulder when they returned to the kitchen.

He'd told her on more than one occasion to make herself at

home whenever she visited. "Not at all. I was thinking about doing that anyway. I'll grab some milk and sugar."

Priscilla set the French press on the table and went back to get some mugs. "Jordan turned out to be much different than I expected."

"You and me both, Mom. I really expected someone like Brad to show up today," Taylor said, pulling her chair out. "Did either of you see any similarities between him and Reese?"

He hadn't seen any family resemblance between the two. But then again, his brain might have been only letting his eyes see what he wanted them to.

"I didn't see any," Priscilla answered.

"Yeah, neither did I. Curt, what about you?"

Curt shook his head as he poured coffee into all three mugs.

"And Jordan said she looked like Eliza, so maybe he didn't see one either," Priscilla pointed out.

As much as it pleased him to know none of them thought Reese shared any traits with Jordan, he knew the lack of a family resemblance didn't prove anything. Although he looked a great deal like his dad and many of his cousins, his older brother, Brett, took after their mom's side of the family.

"For now, I guess all we can do is keep our fingers crossed." Priscilla added some milk and sugar to her coffee before taking a sip. "What time is Judith bringing Reese home?"

"Around six," Taylor answered.

"Good. Then I have time to bring up the decorations and start wrapping Christmas presents."

"If you want, we'll come over and help you," Curt offered. He wasn't much into decorating for the holidays, but after last year he knew how much Reese, Taylor, and Priscilla enjoyed it. And if he required any reminding of that fact, all he needed to do was go in his basement where all the decorations they used in his house last holiday season waited to be used again this year.

"That would be great."

SIX

ALTHOUGH STILL IN ELEMENTARY SCHOOL, Reese had reached a point where she missed a lot when not in class, so Taylor preferred not to dismiss Reese early from school. Today there had been no way around it. The laboratory didn't offer evening appointments, and the first early morning one they had available wasn't for another week. Since she refused to wait until then to bring Reese in for a cheek swab, she took the first opening they had, a two o'clock appointment Monday afternoon.

"Why did you pick me up early, Auntie?" Reese asked as they exited the building and walked toward the school's parking lot.

"Because we're going to Boston."

During breakfast, Taylor let Reese know she'd be picking her up from school so that they could go into Boston. She hadn't gone into all the details of why. While highly unlikely, she'd hoped Reese wouldn't ask for more information.

Reese tossed her backpack in the car and then climbed in after it. "I know. You told me that. But why? Are we doing something for the wedding?"

When Taylor and Curt looked at the Harbor House, the

establishment they'd picked for their wedding reception, they'd taken Reese with them. She'd also taken Reese along when she'd gone shopping for the bridesmaids' dresses. Given those two things, Reese's guess now made perfect sense. And she wished the wedding was the reason for their trip into the city this afternoon.

Putting the car in reverse, she checked the rearview mirror before backing out of the parking spot. "No, we're not doing anything for the wedding. We have an appointment at a lab."

Silence came from the back seat, and Taylor mentally kicked herself for not giving Reese all the details either last night or this morning over breakfast, because the lack of chatter meant Reese was thinking. When Reese started thinking, questions or comments soon followed.

"Is it a lab like the one next to Dr. Baker's office?"

"Similar but not exactly the same."

The laboratory next door to Reese's pediatrician collected blood and urine samples and ran tests for all the physicians in the complex. Although they served different purposes, both facilities collected samples and conducted tests, which meant Taylor wasn't lying.

More silence filled the car. This time, though, it didn't last quite as long.

"Is there going to be a needle?" Reese asked. "I don't want anyone taking my blood."

Like most children, Reese hated getting shots. In fact, Taylor had to hold Reese on her lap whenever she got a vaccine at the doctor's office. During her last physical, though, Dr. Baker had sent Reese over to the lab for routine blood work. It wasn't an event either of them cared to remember or go through again.

"No needles."

"Promise?"

"I promise. You won't see any needles, and no one will take

your blood. If you want when we're done, we can stop at Ambrosia before we go home."

Reese loved stopping at the Ambrosia Café located in Boston. Actually, she enjoyed stopping in any of the Ambrosia Cafés, but the one in Boston was the closest to them since the other two were both in Rhode Island.

"Can we get something to bring home to Curt?"

"Whatever you want." *Please just don't ask me any more questions.*

She heard Reese unzip her backpack. When she didn't say anything else as Taylor headed toward I-93, she assumed Reese had started reading. Unlike Taylor, who became sick if she tried to read even a text message while in a moving vehicle, Reese could read for hours while in the car.

Either Reese finished the book, or she started thinking about their destination again, because before Taylor reached the highway, she asked, "Why do we need to go to a lab? I already had my physical, and I'm not sick."

Taylor had tried to come up with a reasonable excuse in case Reese asked this very question. The only plausible one had been to tell Reese the lab was checking to see if she had any allergies. Ellie, one of Reese's close friends, had recently learned she was allergic to the lactose found in milk products, so her niece might not find the excuse too strange. But one, she hated lying to Reese, and two, her niece might wonder why all of sudden Taylor was worried about allergies when nothing she ate ever bothered her.

"Do you remember what DNA is?"

In July, Reese had attended a two-week science camp. The instructors had all been certified science teachers, and they'd used experiments and other hands-on activities to cover several topics. One of the activities had been to build a representation of the DNA double helix using toothpicks, marshmallows, and gumdrops.

"It's the stuff in your cells that makes you who you are."

"The lab we're going to today is going to collect some of your cells so that they can look at your DNA."

"And they're not going to use a needle, right?"

Taylor took the exit onto the highway, glad that thanks to the time of day at least she didn't have to worry about traffic in addition to Reese's questions. "Nope. They're going to rub a swab against the inside of your mouth. It won't hurt. I promise."

"Why does someone want to look at my DNA?"

Yep, I knew that was coming next. As much as Taylor disliked changing diapers, at the moment, she wished Reese was still the one-year-old baby she'd taken custody of, because then they wouldn't need to be having this conversation.

"When you were with Judith on Saturday, Curt, Mimi, and I met with a man who thinks he might be your father. Once people at the lab have some cells from you and him, they can compare them and determine if Jordan is your dad."

"I don't need a dad. I have Curt."

My sentiments exactly. "And that won't change. But if Jordan is your biological father, he deserves to know." She'd told herself the same thing over a hundred times, yet her head and heart were still in disagreement.

"Do I have to live with him if he is my dad? I want to live with you and Curt."

"No matter what, you'll live with us. But if the results come back and Jordan is your dad, you might need to spend some time with him. For now, I don't want you to worry about any of this."

Until they received a definitive answer, either way, she'd keep doing enough of that for both of them.

SEVEN

Curt opened the door before his brother rang the doorbell. A moment or two later, Honey joined him in the foyer to welcome their guest.

"Love the addition to the yard." Brett pointed toward the inflatable snowman on display.

Although the last day of November, the temperatures were remarkably mild. So after typing the magic words "the end" earlier in the day, he'd decided to take advantage of the nicer weather and put up the exterior decorations. Reese had seen the inflatable snowman that also lit up during a trip to 38 Lumber and Hardware in October and asked him to get it. After he finished setting the snowman up, he'd put up the lights he'd used last year and hung the wreath on the door.

"Your idea or Reese's?"

"What do you think?"

Brett closed the door and shrugged off his jacket. "I think she has you wrapped around her little finger."

His brother wasn't wrong. "More like her entire right hand. Where's Jen?" The last time they spoke, Brett and his fiancée were coming up together today.

"She went out with some friends she used to work with. It was a last-minute thing. Who's the new addition?" Brett rubbed his hand across Honey's head. When he stopped, the dog nudged him in the thigh.

"Honey. I adopted her in September. She likes attention," Curt said as he walked down the hall toward his living room.

"Another of Reese's ideas?"

"This one was all mine, but she adores the dog. Already she plans to have Honey sleep with her when she moves in. And thankfully, Honey and Reese's cat get along."

Brett looked around the room before sitting down in Reese's favorite armchair. "I think you need a housekeeper."

Since he'd gone into the basement to get the exterior decorations, he brought up the boxes of interior ones as well. At the moment, those, along with some containing Taylor and Reese's belongings, were stacked around the room. In Curt's opinion, it was a little cluttered but not a mess. But he knew to his brother, who'd spent most of his adult life in the military, this was utter chaos.

"About half these boxes are decorations. Another quarter of them contains Reese's stuffed animal collection. I didn't want to bring them upstairs until we finished setting up her room." The girl owned enough stuffed animals to open her own store at this point.

"Where is Reese? Since it's nice out, I figured she'd want to give me another soccer lesson. I even brought my sneakers with me."

Much like when he'd first met Reese, she'd offered to give Brett soccer lessons after she found out he'd never played. And like him, Brett had been unable to say no.

Not unexpectedly, Honey followed Curt over to the sofa. As soon as he sat down, the dog jumped up next to him and rested her head on his thigh. Honey loved human companionship more than any dog he'd ever met. "Reese and Taylor had an appointment at Mass Genetics at two. Hopefully, they'll be home soon."

"Is everything okay?"

For the next few minutes, Curt explained the situation to his brother as he ran his hand up and down the dog's back.

Resting his ankle on his knee, Brett leaned back in the chair. "That's crazy. Why would Eliza contact this man now?"

"To make Taylor's life difficult." He had no proof, but what other reason could she have for doing something now that she'd had over nine years to do? "Maybe mine too."

"Does Reese know any of this?"

Curt shook his head. Sunday night he'd suggested Taylor tell Reese everything. Not only was the girl smart, but she also was curious. Reese would want to know why someone stuck a swab inside her mouth and rubbed it against her cheek. If Taylor didn't tell her the truth beforehand, she'd have to lie when Reese brought it up. He knew all too well how a simple lie could come back and bite you in the ass.

"Taylor wanted to wait for the test results," Curt explained, checking his watch. Taylor had told him the appointment shouldn't take long. Unless they either hit traffic or made a stop somewhere else after they left the lab, they should be home soon. "As if the situation didn't suck enough, I talked to Taylor about adopting Reese. She was all on board. I was literally seconds away from asking Reese how she felt about the idea when Taylor's mom called and asked her to come home because she'd gotten the phone call from Jordan."

Brett let out a low whistle. "You never mentioned you were thinking about doing that. But I suspected you might."

"There's a good chance it won't happen now."

"Then you think Jordan is Reese's father?"

"Honestly, I don't know. I didn't see any resemblance, but that doesn't mean anything. No one would guess you and Dad are related. And look at Callie. The only thing she inherited from Uncle Warren is her eye color."

"Even if it turns out Jordan is Reese's father, that doesn't mean adoption is off the table. It's not like he has a relationship with Reese. He might be willing to walk away and let you adopt her."

Curt wished he believed that was a possibility. "If you found out you had a nine-year-old daughter, would you let another man adopt her?"

"Hell no," Brett answered immediately. "But—"

"I didn't get the impression Jordan would either." Curt stood up, and as if attached to him, Honey did the same thing. "I'm going to get a drink. Do you want something?"

"Yeah, sure, whatever you're having," Brett answered, following him and Honey from the room.

After handing his brother a bottle of beer, he took a long drink from his and then went in search of a snack. Before he found anything he felt like eating, the doorbell rang.

"You make Taylor ring the bell?" Brett asked.

Curt sent his brother a dirty look as he walked by him. "It's probably Aaron."

"Aaron?"

"You know, Aaron Wright, as in Juliette's boyfriend. You met him at Allison's wedding. Either your old age is catching up, or all the time you spend with politicians these days is causing serious memory loss."

Even after nearly a year, Curt still had a hard time wrapping his head around the fact his older brother was a United States Senator, a position he'd expected either of his cousins Trent or Sara to maybe one day hold but not Brett. And he loved to give his brother a hard time about it every chance he got.

"Although that might be a good thing. If I had to spend time with Senators Beck and Marshall, I want to forget things too,"

A BILLIONAIRE'S LOVE

Curt added, referring to two current senators who also happened to be their dad and uncles' longtime friends.

"I know who Aaron is. But why is he here? Isn't Avon over two hours away?" Brett walked with Curt down the hall toward the main foyer.

"He called yesterday and asked if he and Juliette could use my place in Newport this weekend. Since he was working in Boston today, he'd said he'd stop by and pick up the key on his way back home."

He'd been one of the first in the family to meet Aaron in the spring, and since then, he'd spent a fair amount of time around not only Aaron but also his mom, younger sister, and niece. Although not at all the type of man Curt had imagined his younger cousin ending up with, he really liked Aaron. More importantly, Juliette appeared happier than he'd seen her in a long time. Curt suspected it was only a matter of time before Aaron proposed.

"Hey, Aaron, come on in," Curt greeted after opening the door.

"It's a good thing Tiegan is not with me. When the Halloween decorations were out, she begged me to get a giant inflatable pumpkin for the front yard. Now she's asking for a Santa Claus one like her friend has. If she saw that, she'd bug me about it even more. I'll put up lights, but I'm not getting one of those." Aaron gestured toward the snowman before entering the house.

"Maybe I should write that down so I can pull it out and remind you when I see big Cupid outside your house in February," Curt said as he started back toward the kitchen.

"Ignore my brother, Aaron. He's jealous that you can withstand an attack by a little girl and he can't."

Curt acted as though he hadn't heard his brother's comment and retrieved his beer from the counter when they entered the

47

kitchen. "When are you and Juliette planning to leave for Newport?"

"I'm hoping I can convince her to go Thursday night. Her last dance class ends at six. She doesn't teach on Fridays, but she usually spends the day at the studio in the office."

"For some reason, I thought going to Newport was her idea. Good luck keeping her out of the studio on Friday." He'd never seen his cousin as driven as she'd been since opening a dance school in the fall.

"No, she has no idea of what I have planned."

As tempting as it was to ask what Aaron had planned, Curt kept his mouth shut, although he suspected he knew what the answer would be. "Use the place as long as you want," he said, tossing the extra set of keys he'd shoved in his pocket earlier to Aaron. "Do you want anything to drink?"

Aaron pointed toward the bottle in Brett's hand. "One of those would—"

"Curt, we're home. Who's here?" Reese's voice reached them from down the hallway, announcing she and Taylor were there.

Since she'd find out soon enough, he didn't bother to call out a reply. Instead, he grabbed a beer for Aaron while he waited for Taylor and Reese to join them.

Reese entered the room, a pastry box in her hands. When she spotted his brother and Aaron, she immediately smiled. "Hi, Brett." Without any hesitation, she hugged his brother. Over the past year and a half, she had developed a loving relationship not only with his parents but also with his older brother and younger sister.

"Are those for me?" Brett asked, pretending to reach for the box when Reese released him.

"Nope. We got some cannoli, cookies, and tiramisu for Curt." She held on to the box while she went over to hug Aaron. "Is Tiegan here?"

A BILLIONAIRE'S LOVE

The very first time Reese and Aaron's niece met, they hit it off. Now, they regularly sent each other text messages, and often when he and Taylor went up to visit his cousin and her boyfriend, Reese came along so she could hang out with Tiegan.

"Not today," Aaron answered, returning Reese's embrace.

"Next time you come, please bring her too. I want to show her my new room. Curt let me pick out the color for the walls and help him paint. And last week, my new furniture came. It's all ready for me to move into after Curt and Auntie's wedding."

"I'll do my best," Aaron promised.

"Here, Curt. Aunt Taylor and I went to Ambrosia after our appointment. These are for you." Reese handed him the box and made a beeline for the refrigerator.

"Thanks, short stuff."

"I think he should share. What do you think, Reese?" Brett asked.

Reese poured a large glass of milk while she considered the question. "We did get everything for him, but I share stuff with my friends. Maybe he should give you and Aaron a tiny piece."

"There's enough in there for us all to have more than a tiny piece," Taylor said.

"If everyone has some, can I have something too?" Reese asked, looking at him instead of Taylor.

Taylor didn't give him a chance to reply. "You already had an enormous cupcake, my friend. You don't need any more sweets right now. And while you wait for dinner, go start your homework."

"Fine," she grumbled before glancing at him again. "Please save me a cookie."

"I'll save you two cookies." Curt ruffled her hair and set the box on the table.

While he waited for Reese to leave the room, he got some plates and forks. He'd never get his brother to leave without sharing some of the pastry. "How did everything go today?"

49

"Okay. The appointment didn't take long. We would've been home sooner, but we stopped at the café and then hit traffic." As he'd known she would, Taylor selected a slice of tiramisu from the sweets on display. Rather than sit down and eat, though, she added water to the French press. "And Reese asked questions about why we were going to the lab."

He'd known she would. "What did you tell her?"

"The truth."

"Was she upset?" Put in Reese's shoes, he had no idea how he'd respond.

"Upset? No, I wouldn't say that. But she wasn't happy either. She told me she doesn't need a dad because she has you."

Curt never doubted how much Reese cared about him. Still, happiness expanded in his chest, and he swallowed down the emotion choking him. "Did you hear back from Jordan?"

"I got a message from him before I picked Reese up at school. The lab in Concord has an opening tomorrow morning, so he's going before work."

The lab assured them results within three to six days, so they'd at least have the truth soon. Curt just hoped it was the news he wanted.

EIGHT

EARLY SATURDAY EVENING, Curt watched as Reese and Erin, Leah's stepdaughter, helped the four boys playing with the plastic blocks. The day before, Taylor, Priscilla, his sister, and several of his female relatives, including his mom, had driven up to Ravenwood Ski Resort for Taylor's bachelorette party—a party his sister had planned. With the women gone, the men had descended on his house for the day and brought plenty of toys to keep the boys occupied. Reese added to the collection by bringing over a farmhouse complete with plastic animals she'd played with at their age and Taylor had never thrown out.

Tomorrow the women would take over childcare duty while the men headed into Salem for his bachelor party at the Ultimate Escape. He'd visited a similar establishment over the summer with Taylor, Reese, and Reese's friend Hazel. Even though they'd failed to solve the puzzles and escape, they'd had a great time. He expected tomorrow to be just as enjoyable.

"Maybe I should hire them as babysitters," Dylan Talbot, a longtime family friend and his cousin's husband, said. "James doesn't want to nap anymore and constantly wants Callie's attention."

"It's hit or miss getting Garrett to nap these days too," Jake commented.

Across the room, Reese handed James, who'd turned three in the fall and was the oldest of the group, a bright yellow block. From the moment the boys had arrived, Reese and Erin had stuck close to them and helped keep them all occupied as well as out of trouble. If and when he and Taylor had children, he had no doubt Reese would be a wonderful older sister. Judging by what he'd seen today, he'd say the same thing about Leah's stepdaughter.

"Sounds like he needs a sibling or two." His cousin, Scott, picked up his almost seven-month-old daughter, who'd crawled over to him.

Belinda had been wearing a purple top and black bottoms when they'd arrived, while her identical twin, Theresa, wore a striped top and blue bottoms. Sometime after lunch, both girls had needed new outfits, and now Curt didn't know if Scott was holding Belinda, who they'd named after Paige's aunt Bebe, or Theresa, who they'd named after Scott's maternal grandmother. Even though his cousin had admitted he occasionally got them confused, Curt didn't want to ask Scott which daughter was now on his lap.

"Or two? We're not all overachievers like you, Scott. Most of us go the one baby at a time route." Jake picked up Scott's other daughter, who'd made her way over to them, and settled her on his lap.

At the moment, Scott had the most children, but Curt suspected it wouldn't be long before his other cousins started adding to their families. Of the men gathered around him, he expected Trent to announce his wife was expecting first. Both Trent and Addie came from large families, and his cousin had told him that was what they both wanted. But he didn't think Jake would be far behind.

Scott shrugged and readjusted his daughter on his lap. "Don't knock it until you try it. The pure chaos in my house these days is like nothing you've ever experienced."

With three children under the age of three, Curt could only imagine what Scott's day-to-day life was like these days.

"He's not lying. I've seen it firsthand," Dylan added. Although Dylan and his wife spent most of their time at their estate in Connecticut, both he and Scott worked at Sherbrooke Enterprises Headquarters in New York City and often visited each other.

"Did you and Nicole finalize the new custody agreement?" Curt asked while he looked for any differences between Scott's two daughters that would help him determine who was who in the future.

Until recently, Scott and his ex-girlfriend had shared custody of their son, although it had seemed like Cooper spent far more time with Scott than his mother—a situation he knew his cousin preferred. Still, Curt had been speechless when Scott shared that Nicole had decided it would be better for her marriage, career, and Cooper, in that order, if Scott had sole custody of their son.

"Two weeks ago. Our lawyers worked it out so that Nicole has Cooper one weekend a month. If she wants and I agree, she can take him for more than one. She is also allowed to take him on vacation for up to ten days three times a year. But if Nicole said she wanted to take him for thirteen days, I wouldn't say no."

He couldn't fathom putting his career before his child, but then Scott's ex didn't strike him as the maternal sort either. Although he'd only met Nicole Sutton once, he had seen stories about the actress. The woman enjoyed the limelight, and at least prior to her marriage, she had been willing to sleep with anyone if it would somehow benefit her career. In fact, she'd been sleeping with Alastair Corey, a well-known movie director, for that reason while still dating Scott. And if that weren't bad enough, she'd also been seeing her current husband at the same time, which was why when Cooper was born, she'd been unsure of who his father was.

"Any word on your, uh, situation?" Scott glanced toward Reese and Erin, who appeared far more focused on the little boys in the room than the adults.

"What kind of situation did Curt get himself into this time?" Trent asked as he pulled his cell phone from his pocket.

Other than his parents, only Scott and Brett knew about Jordan and the pending paternity test.

"Has he been pretending to be someone else again?" Trent continued, alluding to Curt's actions when he'd first moved to Pelham and hadn't been completely honest with his neighbors about who he was. At the time, both Trent and Gray had warned him his lack of honesty might blow up in his face. Thankfully, Taylor had been understanding and willing to forgive him when the truth came out.

Reese approached the group holding Garrett's and Kendrick's hands before he could answer. "Curt, the boys want a snack. Erin and I do too. Can we get something in the kitchen?"

Since he did not know what types of foods were suitable for two- and three-year-old children, he'd asked Taylor for suggestions when he found out he'd be having visitors this weekend. Now, his kitchen had everything from graham crackers and Cheerios to goldfish and yogurt pouches.

"As long as it's okay with them, get whatever you want and bring it in here." He nodded in the general direction of the dads. He didn't care about the children having a snack, but his cousins might feel differently.

Once they received the okay, Reese and the boys headed toward the doorway. Erin soon followed her with James and Cooper.

Scott stood up as his son and Erin passed by him. "If you'll watch Bebe, I'll go help them. They might need it."

"Yeah, of course." Curt accepted Scott's daughter and made

a mental note to remember Belinda was wearing the brown onesie with the large pink poodle on the front.

Trent waited until the children and Scott left before circling back to the conversation they'd been having. "What kind of situation have you gotten yourself into this time?"

Curt gave them the condensed version of events over the past week.

"When will you and Taylor find out?" Jake asked when he finished.

"Soon. Both Jordan and Reese had the cheek swabs done at the beginning of the week," he answered, reaching for his beeping cell phone on the end table.

We're all on our way back. The message from Taylor read.

He'd expected them much later tonight. He knew his sister had made dinner reservations at The Raven's Nest, the nicest restaurant at the ski resort. While Leah could have changed their reservation time, he didn't see why she would. If the group was on its way home now, either Leah had changed it or something had happened. But then again, if someone in the group was injured, one of his cousins would've received a phone call or a text message. Other than when his younger cousin Alec called earlier to let his brother Trent know he wouldn't be up today but would see everyone tomorrow in Salem, everyone's phone had been silent up until now.

Is everything okay?

Curt received a response right away.

I received an email from the lab.

Mass Genetics told Taylor they'd email the results to both her and Jordan. When they didn't arrive yesterday, he'd assumed the lab was closed on the weekends and they wouldn't hear anything until Monday at the earliest.

Taking in a deep breath, he exhaled slowly before replying. **And?**

I'm waiting until I get home to check. That's why we're on our way back. See you soon.

You can read the results without me.

I'd rather wait.

Setting the device down, Curt rested his head against the back of the armchair and closed his eyes.

"Bad news?" Brett pulled his beeping cell phone from his pocket and looked at the screen.

"Taylor got the results from the lab."

"Since you aren't smiling, I guess it means Jordan is Reese's father," his brother said as he typed a message and then put his phone away.

He both understood Taylor's reasoning and appreciated that she was waiting until they were together to read the results. At the same time, he wished she'd opened the email as soon as she saw it and put him out of his misery. "Taylor hasn't read the email yet."

"I would've opened it as soon as I saw it," Brett said.

"She's waiting until she gets home. Everyone is on their way back now."

"Yeah, I just got a text from Jen telling me they'd be home in about two hours."

Reese and Erin reentered the room and escorted the boys over to the large coffee table. Scott followed them, carrying a tray of drinks and snacks for both the adults and the children. "I thought they had dinner reservations," Scott said.

"Small change in plans." Curt snagged a can of root beer as his cousin walked by and opened it. At the moment, he'd much prefer a shot or two of scotch, but with eight children in the house, soda would have to do.

He watched Reese pour some goldfish into a plastic bowl for James, then stick a straw in his juice box. And for at least the twentieth time this week, he prayed the test determined that Jordan and Reese weren't related.

NINE

THE PREVIOUS AFTERNOON, they'd arrived at Ravenwood around dinnertime. While Taylor, Leah, and Taylor's two cousins settled into Leah and Gavin's mountainside condo, the rest of the group checked into their rooms at the ski resort's hotel. Then, before they all headed out for some nighttime skiing, she'd checked her email one last time for the day. And bright and early this morning, Taylor had checked it again before heading out for a day on the slopes. She'd almost not bothered to open her email app when she'd returned to the condo to change before everyone met up at The Raven's Nest for dinner. But after showering, she grabbed her cell phone, more out of habit than because she expected to find anything. When she saw the email address, her first instinct had been to open the message and know once and for all the truth. Instead, she'd closed the app, explained why she wanted to skip dinner, and asked if anyone minded. Not surprisingly, no one had, since everyone there knew the situation.

"I think my brother would understand if you read the report without him." Leah glanced at her from the driver seat as they waited for the traffic light to turn green.

As if to torture herself, she'd logged into her email account at least half a dozen times since leaving Ravenwood. Now, just like every other time, the subject line taunted her. With one simple touch, she could read the results and find out if Jordan was Reese's father.

Don't do it. Taylor's finger hovered over the email. Instead of opening it, she logged out of her account, flipped her cell phone over, and went back to looking out the car window. They were almost to Curt's house. After waiting this long, she could hold out for another five or ten minutes.

"I know, but I want to wait."

Taylor had her reasons for not reading the results now. Perhaps most importantly, she and Curt were a family, and some things needed to be done as a family. Her second reason for not checking was because if the results weren't the ones she wanted, Taylor wasn't sure how she'd react, and she'd rather not embarrass herself in front of the people in the car.

Lillian, her maid of honor and cousin, leaned forward and patted her shoulder from the back seat. "You've got more self-discipline than me. I would've opened it two hours ago."

"Since you haven't heard from Jordan, it might mean he's not the father," Jen, Curt's future sister-in-law, said.

"Or he hasn't checked his email today." Not everyone checked their accounts every day. Some people, like her mom, opened their account only two or three times a week.

After turning onto Route 38, Leah stopped again as they approached a line of traffic, something that rarely occurred on this stretch of the road unless there was an accident. "Is there another way home?"

Of all the days. "Not a good one. Even if we wait in this, we'll still get home quicker than if we go the other way."

"Do you think Curt's house is still standing?" Lillian asked as a way to distract her.

With eight children, several of them still in diapers, and only seven adults, the men had had their hands full today. Taylor knew both Reese and Erin would help in any way the men might need, except for maybe changing a dirty diaper. Still, even with the added assistance, the house might have become a little crazy.

"If it's not, my brother will have something to work on after the honeymoon," Leah replied.

"Brett probably had all of them except Theresa and Belinda running laps and doing pushups," Jen said.

Leah shook her head. "Nah, I bet Reese convinced Curt to move the furniture so they could play soccer in the house. She has my brother wrapped around her little finger. He can't say no to her."

Knowing all the parties involved, Taylor could picture discovering either scenario when they arrived at Curt's home.

When she walked in the house ten minutes later, the smell of pizza and popcorn greeted them rather than screaming children and crying grown men.

"From here, the house looks okay." Leah stopped next to her and shrugged off her jacket.

"That's because Kendrick and Garrett are busy using markers to redecorate the kitchen walls," Jen said, coming up on the other side of her.

It wouldn't surprise Taylor if Jen turned out to be right. As much as she adored the two little boys, when they got together, everyone better watch out.

"Those two are just like Trent and Jake were at that age," Judith added. She'd pulled into the driveway a moment or two after they had.

"Again, it'll give my brother something to do when you return from your honeymoon," Leah said.

Unsurprisingly, Curt met the group in the hallway before they reached the living room.

"Since I doubt you guys saved us any pizza, I'll order us something to eat," Leah offered before she and the other women continued on down the hall.

Taking her hand, Curt led her back toward the foyer in silence.

"I half expected to find a soccer game going on when I walked in."

"We did that before lunch, so we'd have time to move the furniture back."

She couldn't tell from his tone if he was being serious or not.

Opening the library door, Curt switched on the lights and let her enter the room first. "You didn't have to wait for me." He closed the door behind him, although why, she didn't know. With everyone in the living room, no one would hear them in here.

"I wanted us to read it together. Did you say anything to Reese about me getting the results?"

He shook his head as he sat down. "It seemed pointless to mention it until we knew one way or the other."

Since the last time Taylor looked, she'd received emails from three other individuals. She didn't even check the subject lines. They'd all be there later.

She scanned the brief standard cut-and-paste message before scrolling down to the attached report and opening it. Next to her, Curt remained silent, his leg rubbing against hers as he bounced his knee up and down while he waited.

After reading the results a second time, she bowed her head and collapsed against the sofa.

"What does it say?"

"Jordan is not Reese's father."

"Are you sure?"

She handed Curt the cell phone, so he could read the report himself. And as he did, she watched the tension leave his body.

"We should tell Reese and Mom."

Her niece didn't know she'd received the results, but Mom and everyone else who'd gone skiing with her this weekend did. And they were almost as anxious as she'd been to learn the truth.

A BILLIONAIRE'S LOVE

"Let's talk to Reese first. But I need to grab something before we do. While I'm up, I'll get Reese and bring her in here." He kissed her cheek before standing up. "Be right back."

Whether they told Reese alone or Reese and Mom at the same time didn't matter to her. For some reason, Curt cared, so she didn't argue with his suggestion. However, she was darn curious about why it mattered and what he needed to get before they spoke to Reese.

"Curt went upstairs. He'll be right back," Reese said, entering the room. "How come you're home so early? I thought you weren't going to be back until after I went to bed, and that was why I was sleeping here tonight."

"We decided to skip dinner and come home early because—" She stopped when Curt came in and closed the door again.

He put down the gift in his hand before joining her. She'd noticed the present sitting on his nightstand. Although not wrapped in the same snowman wrapping paper as the other presents Curt had wrapped so far, she had assumed it was a Christmas present for someone.

"Because why?" Reese asked.

"The laboratory we went to for the DNA test emailed me the results. I came home so that Curt and I could check them."

"Oh." Frowning, Reese dropped into a chair and crossed her legs in front of her. "Is that why Curt got me? So you guys can tell me what it says." She rested both elbows on her legs and propped her chin in her hands.

Taylor nodded. "Jordan, the man I told you about on Monday, isn't your father."

Reese's transformation was like nothing she'd ever seen. Jumping to her feet, she turned toward the door. "I need to tell Erin and Mimi."

"Hold up, short stuff. I have a present I want you to open first," Curt said.

At the word "present," Reese spun around. "But it's not

Christmas yet, and it's too early to be for my birthday." Despite the apparent confusion, she accepted the small box without complaint.

"It's not a Christmas present. It's something I bought for you, and I want you to open now."

Her niece didn't need any additional instructions. She tore off the silver bow and placed it on Curt's head before ripping off the purple paper. The box's cover soon landed on the floor next to the wrapping paper, and Reese pulled a white gold ID bracelet out.

"It looks like Hazel's, but hers is yellow and has a heart charm on it."

Around Halloween, Reese had mentioned that she wanted a bracelet like Hazel's. Although Taylor hadn't purchased one yet, she'd planned to buy her one for Christmas. It looked like Curt had beat her to it.

Rather than ask Curt or Taylor to put it on her wrist, Reese handed the bracelet back to Curt. "Curt, the store gave you the wrong one. My initials are R.E.W. The ones on here are R.E.S."

Now she understood why he hadn't asked Mom to join them.

Smiling, Curt took both of Reese's hands in his. "They didn't give me the wrong one, short stuff. Your name right *now* is Reese Emma Walker, but if it's okay with you, I'd like it to be Reese Emma Sherbrooke."

Reese tilted her head slightly to the left as her eyebrows bunched together. "For us to have the same last name, you'd have to adopt me. Like Megan's parents did, but they adopted her when she was a little baby, and Megan doesn't remember it happening. And if you adopted me, then you'd be my dad."

"Correct on both accounts, if it is something you want."

Grabbing the bracelet back, she launched herself at Curt. "Can I call you Dad?"

Wrapping his arms around her, Curt kissed Reese's cheek. "You can call me Curt or Dad. It's up to you."

Taylor had fallen in love with him over a year and a half ago when he showed up with a lacrosse stick in each hand, ready to give Reese a lesson. Now with him sitting there with a silver bow on his head and making her niece the happiest girl in the world, judging by her smile, Taylor fell in love with him all over again.

"Will you help me put this on?" Moving from Curt's embrace, Reese handed Curt the bracelet and extended her arm out. "Hey, now that you'll be my dad, Leah and Brett will be my aunt and uncle. Do you think they'll let me call them Aunt Leah and Uncle Brett?"

When Curt mentioned adopting Reese, she'd told him he had nothing to worry about. Later, she'd remind him how right she'd been.

Curt fastened the bracelet around Reese's wrist. "I don't know. You'll have to ask them."

Yeah, she didn't see Leah and Brett saying anything but yes. They'd been treating Reese like a niece for over a year.

Reese grabbed Curt's hand, and then as if just remembering Taylor sat there, she took hers too and pulled. "C'mon, let's go ask them and tell Mimi and Erin."

She didn't let go until they reached the living room where everyone was gathered.

"Guess what?" Reese called out, stepping into the room.

Reese's question stopped the various conversations, and everyone, including the four little boys, looked in their direction.

"Curt's going to be my dad, and I'll have the same last name as him and Aunt Taylor."

Her mom blinked several times, but Taylor still noticed a few tears slip down her cheeks. "All good news in the email then?"

Not only good news but perhaps the best news she'd received in a long time. "Yep."

Joining them, Curt's mom hugged Reese. "You do realize if

Curt's your father that makes me your grandmother. And since you already have a Mimi, you'll have to call me Nana."

Reese's face lit up, and she smiled. "I didn't think of that. And it means Jonathan is my grandfather, right?"

Judith nodded.

"What should I call him?" Reese asked.

"You'll have to ask him next time you see him," Judith answered.

Satisfied with the answer, Reese approached Curt's brother. "Can I start calling you Uncle Brett?"

"You better, or I won't play soccer with you anymore." Brett pulled Reese in for a bear hug.

"Same goes for me," Leah called from the opposite sofa.

"You want Reese to call you Uncle Brett?" Trent asked.

Leah threw her cousin a dirty look and elbowed him in the side. "Reese knows what I mean."

In true nine-year-old fashion, Reese rolled her eyes. "Trent, she wants me to call her Aunt Leah." Turning, she glanced at the table where the boys were eating their snack, and then she looked back at Taylor and Curt. "Since Trent, Jake, Scott, and Callie are Curt's cousins, does that mean Kendrick, James, Cooper, and Garrett will be my cousins now?"

"Yep, and so will Theresa, Belinda, and Courtney's son, Liam."

Reese's eyes doubled in size. "I'll have seven cousins. Cool."

"More than that, Reese. You also get stuck with those two." Jake pointed at Trent and Scott before he continued. "As well as Scott's two sisters, Trent's brothers and sister, Callie, Sara, and me."

If someone could pass out from excitement, her niece would be lying on the floor right now. "Awesome."

"We're kinda related now too, since Leah is my stepmom

and she's Curt's sister," Erin called out from where she sat cleaning up the goldfish one of the boys had spilled on the table.

With a smile stretching from ear to ear, Reese joined Erin and hugged her before accepting the graham cracker James offered her.

"Have I ever told you how much I love your family?" she whispered in his ear. How could she not love the people gathered around her? From day one, they'd accepted her, Reese, and Mom into their lives and made it clear they considered them family.

"They're your family now too."

TEN

Some women spent months and months searching for the perfect wedding gown. Not her. About two months after Curt proposed, Taylor stopped into a bridal boutique in Boston during her lunch break. She hadn't walked in expecting to purchase anything. She'd gone in more just to get an idea of the various styles available and, at the same time, get a few ideas of what she might like Reese and the rest of the bridal party to wear. She'd spotted her gown on a mannequin and fallen in love with its simple but elegant design. The moment she slipped it on and saw her reflection, she'd known she'd found *the* gown. Looking at her reflection in the mirror now, she loved the wedding dress even more than the last time she'd put it on for her final fitting.

"Aunt Taylor, you look beautiful," Reese said, putting an arm around Taylor's waist as she joined her again now that the photographer had finished taking pictures.

When she'd asked Reese if she'd like to be a junior bridesmaid in the wedding, instead of saying yes, the first words out of her mouth had been, "Do I have to wear a dress?" While they didn't plan to have anything as formal and elaborate as Allison,

Curt's cousin, had in June, Reese couldn't walk down the aisle in soccer shorts and cleats either.

Rather than complain or flat-out refuse to be part of the wedding if she had to wear a dress when she found out it was required, she'd simply nodded and asked Taylor not to make her wear anything with sequins—a request that was easy to accommodate, since Taylor didn't care for sequins either. Reese hadn't blinked an eye when she found out she'd need to wear tights either.

Nope, the disagreement came when it came to shoes. Reese had wanted to wear her new leopard-print combat boots Curt's mom bought her back in September for school. She'd insisted fancy dress shoes like the ones she'd worn to the party at the White House hurt her feet. Taylor had understood her niece's sentiments. Dress shoes weren't always the most comfortable, and the first chance she got at the reception tonight, she planned to kick off her heels. Still, combat boots didn't go with a bridesmaid's dress.

In the end, Reese had called in reinforcements. At first, when Curt suggested new navy blue, high-top canvas sneakers, Taylor had balked at the idea. While the same color as Reese's dress, they weren't much better than the boots. Then he'd reminded her how they'd both agreed they wanted Reese to enjoy herself today and that she hadn't complained once about wearing a dress and tights. Presented with such a unified front, she'd given in, which was why Reese stood there wearing a navy blue, floor-length chiffon dress with a V-neckline and flutter sleeves as well as blue canvas high tops. Although honestly, for the most part, the full skirt hid her unique footwear.

Mom joined them in front of the mirror, dressed in a plum-colored, floor-length gown with a beaded jewel neckline and three-quarter sleeves. "I think you both look beautiful. Curt's one lucky man."

As far as Taylor was concerned, she and Reese were just as lucky.

"I wish your dad was here to see the two of you." Over the past several months, Mom had made similar statements whenever they spoke about her wedding.

Yep, having Dad there would have been fantastic. But since it was impossible, Taylor refused to dwell on his absence. Instead, she concentrated on the fact two of the most important people in the world were standing next to her, and soon she'd be seeing the third.

"It's not too late, Taylor. You can still make your escape. I can call Sara and ask her to arrange for Christopher's plane to fly you to wherever you want. Then we can have the driver bring you to the airport instead of the church," Leah said as she walked back into the living room.

In a perfect world, Eliza would've organized her bachelorette party and then acted as her maid of honor. But this wasn't a perfect world, and her older sister had made decisions that meant she would never be a part of Taylor's or Reese's life again. That didn't mean Taylor wouldn't have a sister at the altar with her this afternoon. It just meant that the sister wouldn't be biologically related to her.

In the beginning, Taylor had been a little uncomfortable around Curt's sister. That had quickly changed, and now she had a better sisterly relationship with Leah than she'd ever had with Eliza.

"As tempting an offer as it is, I better pass. Your brother would be lost without me."

Leah sighed loudly. "True. I guess that means we better go before Curt drags Reverend Shawn over here. He's probably already tried, and Brett had to tie him to a chair to keep him from doing it again."

An image of Brett tying his brother to a chair after Curt

attempted to pull Reverend Shawn out of the church played through her head. "Do you think Brett used rope or zip ties?"

"Knowing Brett, both. He likes to do things right the first time," Leah answered.

ELEVEN

When he'd rolled out of bed, his stomach contained more knots than the rigging on a sailboat. Somehow, he'd managed to drink the coffee Brett shoved his way. Eating the bacon and eggs his brother, who'd spent the night with him, cooked had been out of the question. He'd expected excitement this morning, not nervousness. After all, what did he have to be nervous about? It wasn't like Taylor would say no rather than I do once she reached the altar. Or that she wouldn't show up at the church.

The arrival of the photographer, his dad, Scott, and Derek, his two groomsmen, had distracted him a little. But even with the other men present, he'd done a fair amount of pacing and time checking. At one point, Dad even poured him a shot of scotch, told him he'd downed one himself right before his wedding, and then ordered him to drink it. It'd helped slightly until they reached the church. Once there, he'd spent his time either looking at his watch or out the window for any sign of Taylor's limo and more or less driving everyone around him crazy.

When Brett put him out of his misery and told him the limo carrying the bridal party had arrived, the knots in his stomach

A BILLIONAIRE'S LOVE

disappeared and a sense of calm descended—not that it lasted long. The moment he saw first Reese and then Taylor escorted by Priscilla come toward him, everything from love to the need to protect assaulted him.

Except for when Jake got married, Curt had attended all of his cousins' weddings. Although Curt would never tell any of them, he'd found them all long, tedious affairs where he spent most of the time thinking about everything from the plot of his book to whether he wanted to use oak or Brazilian cherry hardwood flooring in the dining room of whatever current house he was renovating.

Not so today.

"Taylor and Curt have prepared their own vows today," Reverend Shawn announced to the crowded church. Although they'd only invited family and close friends, there wasn't an empty pew in the 18th-century church.

Although no one else knew it, his wedding vows were not the only ones he'd prepared for this afternoon. In hindsight, he should've given the reverend a heads-up on his plan for today. But it was a little too late now. "Reverend Shawn, before Taylor and I exchange vows, there is something else I need to do."

The reverend's lips parted, and he glanced at Taylor before meeting his eyes again. "Certainly, this day is all about the two of you."

You're mostly correct. Walking past Taylor, Curt took Reese's hand and led her back to where he'd been standing. Then he dropped to one knee, so he was at her eye level and pulled the gold heart pendant necklace from his pocket.

"Reese Walker, soon-to-be Reese Sherbrooke, you and your aunt Taylor captured my heart a long time ago. No matter what, I promise to love you, take care of you, and be the best father I can possibly be." He barely managed to fasten the necklace around her neck before she threw her arms around him.

"I love you too." As quickly as she hugged him, Reese let go and moved back into her spot between Lillian and Leah.

Tears glistened in Taylor's eyes when he rejoined her. "I love you." Although they'd yet to exchange vows, she kissed him.

CURT WATCHED TAYLOR, Reese, and several other wedding guests perform the *Old Town Road* dance. It wasn't a song he would've added to the reception playlist, but both Reese and Taylor liked it. And as long as he didn't have to dance to it, he didn't care if the DJ played it.

"After that vow you made to Reese in the church, you're probably Mom's favorite child," Brett said.

With Taylor dancing, he'd joined his brother and a few of his guests whose companions were on the dance floor.

"Never mind being Aunt Judith's favorite child. He earned brownie points with every one of our female relatives this afternoon. I swear, when he dropped to one knee in front of Reese, every woman in the church was on the verge of tears," Jake said as he reached for his wineglass. "I think even my dad was."

Curt would accept that his aunts and maybe his female cousins had teared up a little, but not Uncle Warren.

"Sara did cry. Then again, it doesn't take much these days. Were Callie and Charlie overly emotional when they were pregnant?" Christopher asked his brothers-in-law, Jake and Dylan.

Jake shook his head. "Charlie had terrible morning sickness, but I don't remember her being emotional."

"Callie just had strange food cravings," Dylan answered.

"Lucky you." Christopher clasped his hands together on the table. "Just so I know if I should bring tissues or not, do you have any emotional surprises planned for your wedding, Brett?"

"I didn't, but now I might need to come up with something so that I can be Mom's favorite son again."

Leah slapped their brother on the arm. "Leave him alone. It is his wedding day." Putting her arm around his shoulders, she kissed his cheek. "What you did was perfect. And you made Reese's day. It was all she could talk about in the limo on the way here."

"Hey, we're only giving you a hard time because we can," Jake commented, looking serious for the first time since Curt joined the group. "Not that it matters. We all adore Reese and thought what you did for her was great."

Before they'd left the church, his brother had pulled him aside and said more or less the same thing. Jake's statement and the nods of agreement it received now didn't surprise him either.

Yep, Jake was right. Still, the way everyone from his mom and dad to his cousins had welcomed her into the family meant a lot to him.

Out on the dance floor, the current song ended. Rather than return to him, Taylor and his cousin Juliette walked off toward where Aaron, who'd proposed to his cousin the weekend they used Curt's house in Newport, Mom, Aunt Marilyn, and Priscilla were sitting. Reese didn't come looking for him either. Instead, she took James, Dylan's son, by the hand and moved back onto the dance floor. Although the youngest generation of Sherbrookes and Belmonts hadn't attended the previous three weddings this year, all of them were there today, even Courtney's son, who had been born in mid-October.

"She's great with children," Leah commented. "You and Taylor have a fantastic future babysitter right there."

He'd thought the same thing on numerous occasions. "Speaking of needing a babysitter, did Alec's date leave?" It took him a moment to locate his younger cousin sitting with their grandmother, Uncle Warren, and Uncle Mark, his cousin's father.

"I saw them having a disagreement in the lobby when I went to the ladies' room," Leah explained, accepting the glass Gavin handed her when he returned from dancing with his daughter, Erin.

"I must admit I feel a little bad for him. He's the only one of us left for Tasha to go after now." Jake's smile conveyed the opposite of sympathy.

The daughter of Richard Marshall, a close friend of his father and uncles, Tasha had gotten it in her head years ago that she wanted to marry into the Sherbrooke family. She didn't seem to care which of the males got her there. Tasha had started by going after Jake. Once he'd been off the market, she'd worked her way down the line. Since they'd limited their guest list to only family members, Curt hadn't invited her or her parents to the wedding. His brother wouldn't be as lucky. Not only did Brett work with Richard now that he was a senator in Washington, but Richard and his wife were close friends of their parents. Whenever events such as weddings or holiday parties took place, the two families included each other.

"Maybe we should hire Alec a bodyguard from Elite Force for Brett's wedding," Curt suggested.

Based in Virginia, the organization provided private security to anyone who could afford them. However, it wasn't all they did. Right after Reese's abduction, he'd hired the firm, and it'd been its Hostile Response Team that found Reese, not the police.

"Not a bad idea. I'll call the firm tomorrow and arrange it." Jake pushed his chair back and stood. "Right now, I'm going to find Charlie and Garrett."

As much as he enjoyed spending time with the people around him, getting his wife in his arms and on the dance floor sounded like a phenomenal idea. "I'll see you all later too."

Taylor, along with the guests seated with her, was laughing when he approached. As soon as they saw him, though, they all fell silent and looked at him.

"We were just talking about you." Judging by Mom's smile,

he didn't want to know what embarrassing story she'd shared with his wife.

Great. After greeting everyone, Curt extended his hand toward Taylor. "Mrs. Sherbrooke, would you like to dance?"

They made it to the edge of the dance floor before he slipped his arms around her waist and pulled her in close.

They moved as one for a moment or two in silence before Taylor spoke. "Reese asked this morning when she'll have a brother or sister."

"Did she?"

"She did. And she said, if possible, she'd like either twin sisters or brothers, so she gets a lot of siblings faster."

"Of course she said that. What did you tell her?" They'd discussed having children at some point, but not when they wanted it to happen.

"That we couldn't promise twins. But hopefully, she'd have a sibling soon."

"How soon were you thinking?" If it were up to him, next year at this time, they'd have a fourth member of their family.

"We're going to be alone for the next week and a half. I say we spend most of that time trying to give Reese what she wants."

"You won't get any argument from me there, Mrs. Sherbrooke." Touching her face, he pressed his lips against hers. When he pulled back, he found her smiling at him.

"I think that should be your new motto. We can have it put on a sign and then hang it over your desk."

"I got a better motto." He lowered his head toward hers again. "I love you." He covered her lips with his before she could answer.

ALSO BY CHRISTINA

Loving The Billionaire
The Teacher's Billionaire
The Billionaire Playboy
The Billionaire Princess
The Billionaire's Best Friend
Redeeming The Billionaire
More Than A Billionaire
Protecting The Billionaire
Bidding On The Billionaire
Falling For The Billionaire
The Billionaire Next Door
The Billionaire's Homecoming
The Billionaire's Heart
Tempting The Billionaire
The Billionaire's Kiss
A Billionaire's Love, a novella
The Courage To Love
Hometown Love
The Playboy Next Door
In His Kiss
A Promise To Keep
When Love Strikes
Born To Protect
His To Protect

One Of A Kind Love, coming June 2021

ABOUT THE AUTHOR

USA Today Best Selling author, Christina Tetreault started writing at the age of 10 on her grandmother's manual typewriter and never stopped. Born and raised in Lincoln, Rhode Island, she has lived in four of the six New England states since getting married in 2001. Today, she lives in New Hampshire with her husband, three daughters and two dogs. When she's not driving her daughters around to their various activities or chasing around the dogs, she is working on a story or reading a romance novel. Currently, she has three series out, The Sherbrookes of Newport, Love on The North Shore and Elite Force Security. You can visit her website www.christinatetreault.com or follow her on Facebook to learn more about her characters and to track her progress on current writing projects.

Printed in Great Britain
by Amazon